GW00393952

Read*ux*

Readux Books: Series 3, No 11

Translation copyright © 2014 by Saskia Vogel

Originally published as
Jag vill veta var stockrosorna kommer ifrån
by Novellix, Stockholm

First English translation, 2014
All rights reserved

ISBN: 978-3-944801-18-6
Cover illustration by Lisa Schweizer
Design by Susann Stefanizen

Published by Readux Books
Sorauer Str. 16, Berlin, Germany

www.readux.net

Where the Hollyhocks Come From

Amanda Svensson
Translated from the Swedish by Saskia Vogel

I want to know where the hollyhocks come from, she said, how they can burst from the asphalt like that, and why grapes can grow along the white limestone walls here, but not oranges, not even lemons as sour as they are, and the cold, why is it relative, people always say that, that it has something to do with the wind and the damp getting into your bones being worse than frost on your eyelashes, she said. Because I don't think so, she said, I think flat landscapes are the most beautiful, along with dry topsoil, scorched earth, and I want to travel south south south as far as you can go, where you can feel the heat against the backs of your thighs when the sun is behind you and where you can sit on up-turned boats during sunrise and you think that it will never be this beautiful again, you know? But of course I didn't know, because the most beauti-ful things haven't happened to me yet, I always imagine them to be in the future, we are differ-ent people in that way, she and I, and I have never seen the Adriatic or the dry earth, just big cities,

5

taxis, clouds of smoke through which beautiful, willing faces emerge and through which greedy hands shoot out, impossible to defend yourself against. Her hands didn't come from the dark of a nightclub, they came through a rosehip hedge, torn up palms, with dirt under her chipped fingernails, her eyes sought my gaze through the foliage, her southern Swedish Rs trilled between the twigs and her rough hair smelled faintly of seaweed and salt water. This is Sweden's southernmost point, did you know that? she said, as if I hadn't a clue, as if I were here by chance, a city dweller like me, and maybe that's how it actually was, by chance, because what was I doing there? My grandmother was on her death bed, but that's never been a legitimate reason for anyone to be anywhere, really, has it? We'd never been close, not even close to being close, but when people die, I thought that this is what you do, so I traveled there to visit her. She lay dying in Sweden's southernmost old age home and that night, I ask her later, that is: her, not grandmother because she'd already died the same night, last night, and I wasn't there because I was busy with something else, I ask her now at the bus stop, that is: her, how she remembers the night at the hostel, the torn sheets and the window with the cobwebs in the corners and the hollyhock along the limestone wall and why she asked me where the hollyhocks come from, as if I would know. Well, because you're from the big city, she says, you should know a thing or two about a thing or two, for example why, on all of Söderslätt, there's only one blackberry thicket and why it happens to grow by the old European Route E4, which makes it impossible to pick the berries unless you want to get run over. Coming from the big city you should know what love is, for instance, you should have a few secrets about garter belts and electrifying discharge, about fruit that never goes moldy. You should know where the hollyhocks come from, and why you can't tell by their seeds which color the flowers will be. But I don't want to talk about that, I don't want to talk in this strange way, so I ask her if she remembers the first night, the only night, last night, how we met near a hedge on Sweden's southernmost headland, in the afternoon, seagulls and sea lyme grass, the sea so close and how she stuck her arm through the hedge and grabbed my arm, which was pale and smooth, hairless and thin, and how her hand ran up my arm and over my shoulder and along my stubbled neck and finally landed on the crown of my head and how she at this point had pulled herself through the hedge of course, with her whole body, because no one has arms *that* long, that I know, and I thought that she was pretty, very pretty, that I remember, but not beautiful, not so it hurts. There's a kind of beauty that hurts, and hers is not that kind, hers is like a cousin's, like a bunny's, like something living that you might like for the moment, but it will never break your heart, make it feel like thousands of glass slivers stuck in a foot, it will never make you miss the bus. She stood there, and my grandmother was on her death bed, and she took me by the waist before I could protest and we walked down towards Sweden's southernmost ice cream stand and bought Sweden's southernmost soft ice cream with licorice sprinkles, and even at that point I don't think that I wanted to make it with her, she wasn't the type, her hair bounced on her shoulders, the only thing I wanted was to sit on Sweden's southernmost pier that she had ferried me to, balancing along a stone wall, a sign pointed in different directions out into the world and it was 1,489 kilometers to Moscow and 658 kilometers to Stockholm, where I'm from, the winters there are milder than here, I said, everyone knows that, it's a different kind of cold up north, it's not as raw as here, and then she laughed at me as little sisters do when they think you're acting like an uncle, when you talk about the weather and they just want to talk about their dreams of the future and their fantasies. I'm twenty-two years old, she said, and I've already been so many places, all of them in that direction, she said and pointed out over the sea, past Sweden's southernmost visible rock and beyond, all south, as far as three hundred kilometers past the equator; once I was in Argentina and rode a horse across the Pampas, and once I was in Granada and plucked salamanders from burning hot stone walls and placed them in the shade to rest, and once I was in southern Turkey and saw a grove of tangerines that stretched endlessly towards the horizon, and once I was in Morocco and drew the scraggly contours of palm trees against the night sky, and all of this I've seen, you understand, I've done all of this but I'm still not satisfied and I still don't know where the hollyhocks come from, because I have a secret that you won't know until it's no longer true. It's a riddle, she said, my secret is a riddle, and while you ponder it you can tell me about the things I haven't seen: fluorescent lights and bar toilets and girls who follow you into them, and what you do with them there, and what their eyes look like after, if they are shining like beautiful glass marbles, if they smolder from within. I said I didn't want to talk about that, I felt it was an inappropriate topic of conversation for people who've just met, and furthermore

9

my grandmother is on her death bed with droop-
ing rapeseed flowers on her nightstand not far away,
but I didn't say this, for some reason I didn't say
this, if I had things would have surely ended dif-
ferently, I could've let it go to begin with, let it go,
but I didn't say anything about my grandmother
and so she didn't say anything about hers, the only
thing I said was that this felt inappropriate and
unpleasant, talking about things like girls I've slept
with, with someone I'd just met, but really it wasn't
the duration of our acquaintance that was the problem, something else was the problem, her eyes with
their strange, hungry shimmer, and her skinned
knees, the dirty Band-Aid on her big toe, the way she
dangled her legs over the pier, the soft ice cream
melting over her hand and how she didn't bother
to wipe it up, just let it drip. The rusty bicycles
with the scratched-up stickers on their frames, horns
instead of bells. She had two, as if she'd been ex-
pecting me, maybe she had been, anyway we didn't
talk about it, the one had a horn that looked like a
tiger, the other like a cat, she gave me the one with
the tiger. Come with me, she said, come with me
and we'll ride across the sea, south; I said that was
a childish statement and she laughed and pulled off
her shirt, and she was almost entirely flat under
there, bra straps soiled by sun and dust, and later,

snot and tiny tears. Anyway, we got on the bikes, she said all-righty-then we'll ride somewhere else, we'll ride to the war, to the memory of the war, to the idea of anti-invasion preparation and so we cycled along the beach path, the wheels were heavy in the sand but it didn't seem like she cared, she was probably used to it, and we arrived at an old bunker, cracked concrete surrounded by sea lyme grass and rusty iron hooks to hold on to while you climbed up it. If you crawl inside you can sleep on a bed of glass and spiders, she said, but you have to pry open the planks first and it's not always worth the trouble, it sort of depends on how you're feeling, right now I think that sitting up top will suffice, there are so many boats out there, I can tell you where they're going. That one's going to Rostock, and that one to Travemünde and that one's just a sailboat, it's not going anywhere special, I've sailed once, through the Grecian isles, Mykonos Naxos Paros and Santorini, kiss me now. I hesitated, she still wasn't wearing her shirt and along one forearm, sticky soft ice cream. She said, they built these bunkers, several hundred along the coast, in anticipation of a war that never arrived, don't you think that's beautiful somehow? In anticipation of boats that would pour in and now they're sitting here like mementos of that which never was, it's

sad, and sometimes I think, she said, just sometimes, that war maybe isn't such a big deal com-
pared with being forced to sit staring day in and
day out over an empty sea where nothing but the
odd fishing boat passes by, and sometimes, kiss me
already. And then I did, because she had moved
so close and I couldn't avoid it, and anyway she had
a look in her eyes that you couldn't say no to, sort
of desperate, almost militant. And I wanted to be
able to love her, for her to be the kind of girl that
you miss your bus for time after time. I wanted her
beauty to hurt, I wanted to want to bite into her
neck, hard, I wanted to tear the planks from the
entrance to the bunker and lay her down on a bed
of glass and spiders, I wanted to want to kiss her
like she'd asked me to, so I did. Kissed her, that is,
not the rest, not then, and not later either, still it
cut like glass, cobwebs in every corner of the window. I ask, do you remember that you asked me
to kiss you? Do you remember that I didn't have
a choice? And she answers that she does remember, of course she remembers that she asked and
how kind of me to agree, how very kind of me, a
disgusting girl like her and I say that it wasn't like
that, it wasn't like that, I tell her she's pretty, but
she doesn't listen. The bus is yellow and is leaving
soon. I have to sort this out before I go, I think,

because I don't like to leave things hanging, scraps of hope, things that can't be catalogued in an orderly fashion like completed projects, I don't like that she's looking at me like I'm tricking her, as if I had been tricking her then, too, in Sweden's southernmost sheets and Sweden's southernmost untouched desert that I couldn't touch, couldn't touch, couldn't—

We have to sort this out now, I say, and ask if she remembers the kiss she practically forced us into. She tasted of black seaweed, south coast seaweed, her teeth were covered in a thin film of salt, and further into her mouth, soft and totally untouched, like sugared marshland, and in the center of her palate a bitterness; this is my bitterness, she said, I haven't kissed anyone since the Scilly Isles, she said as we sat on the bunker, and she made it sound like a long, long time ago. And right then, in that moment, just because her voice was so unspeakably somber, I thought it might almost work, that I would be able to touch her scabby knees, the tanned, flaking skin of her arms, that a flower of an unknown color might yet bloom, the tension created by the fact that at that moment her eyes did have the kind of beauty that hurts, so when she took me by the hand seriously and said, do you want to know my secret I answered yes, even though secrets themselves have never been of interest to me, as little as abandoned vessels of war get my heart going, as little as anything lingers in me. Good, she said, and the somberness vanished, good, you'll find out tomorrow, if you stay the night with me you'll find out, I'll tell you over breakfast, we'll make waffles, and I'll pick blackberries to put on top, you understand, there's a bush and I've never touched it before, but tomorrow I will, and we'll have blackberries on our waffles, and cream that I'll whip, and coffee that you'll brew, with milk that we'll warm, you need two people to warm milk because otherwise it boils over when you're not looking, but if there are two of you, you can take turns blinking and it sorts itself out. We'll stay at the hostel tonight, she said, not at my place, that would be wrong, you know, not at all like I imagined, where there isn't any hollyhock because I've never been able to get it to grow, I don't know where it comes from, no we'll stay at the hostel that looks like a lighthouse, they have dogs there so I hope you're not afraid, are you? They're labradors. Yes, I thought and pressed my palm against the bunker's coarse concrete surface so that it hurt, I am afraid, but not of labradors and that was the question so I said no, not at all, dogs are animals driven by instinct, they don't attack unless you threaten them. Have you

14

ever spent the night in a psychiatric ward? she then asked and I wasn't surprised at all, I'd already given up following the convolutions of her mind, I simply answered no, and she said, me neither, and that was the end of that topic, her eyes: dark charcoal on the dying glow of the fire she made on the beach later, later in the evening, like asphalt, black as asphalt when she said me neither but it sounded like hands clasped in prayer. Black like the labradors that would later bark outside our window in Sweden's southernmost hostel, and shining like silver fur, like the womb's slimy pomade on a newborn puppy's head. Yes, the eyes, for a moment, when they grew so black, like space without stars, for a moment then I thought that she might be beautiful after all, maybe more than a child, maybe I'd be able to—

and I said OK, the hostel tonight, you and me and the sheets and the labradors.

We parted ways later, would meet again at dusk, the same place the same bunker the same crushed glass and spiders, and she would make a fire and I would bring the alcohol, promise you bring the alcohol she said, and her tongue sort of stumbled over the word as if she'd never said it before, the alcohol, and I said yes because I'd already started to get cold feet, already nervous, and only when we parted did I realize that I didn't know where to get any, alcohol that is, out here in the country-side, light beer would have to do but maybe that was just as well, just a child, twenty-two but just a child and already then it was as if something had started to stir in my stomach, a certainty that it wouldn't work, that the sheets would get sweaty for no reason and maybe I already knew her secret, the one that she'd whisper to me while the labra-dors barked madly outside. The moon new, almost invisible and me who couldn't—

but that was later. First I went to see my grand-mother who was in Sweden's southernmost old age home on her death bed, hands clasped lazily be-hind her head as if she were lying on an inflatable pool mattress and not on a hospice cot dressed up as a bed, the county council's pale yellow blanket around her feet, butter-yellow rapeseed in a glass, I went to see her because that's why I was there. She, that is my grandmother, didn't say much. She mostly grinned and scratched her scalp with her pink-painted nails. Lice, it's those damned lice, said grandmother, they're eating through my skull; and even though I knew it was only in her imagi-nation I sort of felt them crawling on my own scalp like invisible fingers, chipped nails, scabs. Do you want to know a secret? asked grandmother with her crazy voice, and I thought what is it with all these secrets, I haven't asked for them but I didn't say that of course, and when it came to it, it wasn't a real secret, just grandmother who came closer and said, I was beautiful once, it's not easy to believe that now, right? But oh I was a beauty, I tell you, more beautiful than your cousin Caroline even, she's more pretty than beautiful really, but she takes after her grandfather, but I was beautiful yes I was, God save me I was, by the way have you met Caroline yet, you do know that she lives here, will you pay her a visit? No, grandmother, I said, you know I've never met Caroline, not even as kids, you know how it is between Mom and Sarah, you know that they haven't spoken for twenty-five years, you know all about it, and grandmother's eyes grew black, like space without stars, like asphalt, black as asphalt, and then she said, that's it, that's it, those girls'll be damned if they can't go on like that, and tore into her scalp again a little and I couldn't take it anymore, her charcoal black eyes, so I just left, just got up and said grandmother I have to go now, I'm meeting someone, but I'll be seeing you okay, I'll be seeing you and I left. This was yesterday but it feels so long ago, now we're sitting at a bus stop, she has bits of seaweed in her hair, she that is, not grandmother, of course not grandmother because she's already dead, bits of black seaweed sort of braided into her coarse yellow wisps, it's not beautiful, it's off-putting and I say this to her, an attack, and she asks if that's why, if she's disgusting, if it's her appearance that's the matter, personally she's always thought that she was quite pretty and if it's that she'd rather like to know what she could change, is it her hair style or is it that she has a hollow between her breasts, that they don't really sit close together so it's like a flat hollow between her breasts, big enough to leave a fingerprint between the right and left, because if that's the problem, then that's it for her, she can't do anything about that, but if it's her hair style that's easy to fix, and I say no, that's not why, it has nothing to do with how you look, another attack, you should wash your hair but that's not why, it wouldn't help and she says oh, is it because of grandmother, if that's why then I understand that it can have shaken you up, how ill she was, is it because you're sad, and I say no, I'm not particularly sad, we've never been close, not even close to being close, and even if I were, sad that is, it wouldn't have mattered, I've done it under worse conditions than this, I'm not that fucking sensitive, that's not how it works. Oh, she says then. Oh. And I realize that I have to say something else, that I can't just leave when her bottom lip is pouting in that childish way, it feels worse now that she's not asking me questions, when she's given up on me being able to explain, just sitting there in silence with one bra strap hanging off her shoulder soiled with snot and tiny tears, and her wrinkled dress and the bus that's getting ready to take me away from here to a bigger city, a station, a train back to women I understand, the kind who don't rub lavender behind their ears instead of perfume, who don't have faded cotton dresses and scabs and crazy voices, who don't know how to wait because they've never had to, who are used to getting what they want, women who don't ask strange things, who don't pick their noses and think no one can see, who know that they're never unseen. But I have to say something, because afterwards she ran straight out into the water, like a black-eyed madman, and I stayed at the window and looked on, unable to do anything, unable in the same way as what happened, and for the first time in my life I was completely unable and not because I knew, because I didn't know then, neither her secret nor what just happened to be a secret because we'd never shaken hands properly, I'd never asked her name and maybe she knew mine or maybe she didn't, I don't know, but anyway I stood there, after the night on the beach, light beer, campfire, her hand so small in mine, how she kept asking me things about the subway system and tattoos, about art museums and cafés and if it really was true that winter nights in Stockholm can get so cold that your nylons freeze to your legs, if it's true that it hurts the first time, and I said what hurts, and she didn't answer and instead started packing everything up, the blanket and the empty cans and the lavender leaves and carried them to Sweden's southernmost hostel. It was indeed a lighthouse with labradors outside, the rooms were very small, in ours there was only a narrow bed and a window, there were spiderwebs in each corner of the window and if you looked out you saw the hollyhock stretching itself up the walls, pink blue purple, even black, and how she talked, she talked and talked, I almost couldn't stand her talking so damn much, babbling, she was probably nervous but I was too, and her babbling didn't help when she let her dress fall, in the end I had to cover her mouth with my hand and then finally she was quiet, and then we both were quiet for hours, until there were tears in the sheets even though nothing had happened, without me being able to even though we tried and tried, it just didn't work, maybe it was because she talked too fucking much to begin with, or it was something else, I couldn't think and I couldn't not think and I finally said, please put your clothes back on, I don't want to anymore please just put some fucking clothes on for fuck's sake, and she did, pulled on her dress and went out and I stayed by the window and watched her go down to the sea, out into the sea, and we hadn't said anything else after my plea for her to get dressed, and now we're sitting here at a bus stop and she wants to know why I couldn't, why I just couldn't give her this one small thing, save her, twenty-two years old but still an unwritten page. Because that's what her secret was, she whispered later, when she came back from the sea disoriented but still alive, she hadn't done it yet, that was her secret, hadn't even gotten close, that was the riddle, she said, and when it wasn't true anymore she would tell, that's how it was supposed to go, and then we were supposed to laugh about it, but it didn't happen like that and suddenly there was nothing to laugh about, and everything was just sad, just so immensely sad. You know, she whispered later, when she'd come back from the sea, I've been so many places, the most beautiful you can imagine, but my own body, my own body is an uncharted continent. No one has ever been here, no one has ever found their way. I've been in the Sahara but my own body is the most deserted landscape I have ever seen. I just want to know what

21

it's like, she said, I want to know if it's like in my fantasies. I want to have something other than Italy to long for, something that smells stronger than the tangerines in Turkey, something more beautiful than the silhouette of palm trees in Morocco. I want to know what the inside of my body feels like, what it looks like, I just want to know what it's like to do it, simply, one single time, is that so fucking much to ask. I want to know what it's like to be a grown person and not just pretty little Caroline.

I don't know if she already knew when she picked me and in that case why she picked me, maybe it was so she could have something to blame, some people work that way, choosing the impossible over the possible every time, some people live in dreams and not in reality because nothing frightens them more than that their dreams might shatter as soon as they are fulfilled, that it will hurt, because it hurts, not just the first time but every time, some people never grow up because they can't stand to see things break, they don't dare, but I don't say this to her, because maybe it wasn't like that, maybe she didn't know, maybe it was just a coincidence, she and me and the bikes, I don't have the energy to ask, I just want to get away from here. But even though she must know that it's impossible, she begs me to stay, says: there are more buses, you could stay a while longer, we could try again. You liked me yesterday, she says, when I came through the hedge, you liked me then, when I touched you and put my hand on your head, when I asked you to kiss me and you kissed me, and when I asked you to spend the night with me and you said you wanted to, you said yes to the hostel and the sheets and the labradors so you must have wanted to, something inside you must have wanted to, so why all of a sudden didn't you want to last night, why don't you want to now, all of a sudden? And I don't know how I should answer, how I should explain the panic, what I should say about the barking dogs, her dress in a heap on the floor and her tense smile, as if I could save her from something, how I should explain how fucking scared I got, and I know that it'd be easy to blame it on the thing that I only understood later, the thing she might have known all along, but it would be a lie because even before I knew how we fit together, I knew it wouldn't work, even before I knew, as we lay in the sheets and it was impossible, actually I knew even earlier, I knew already when the soft ice cream ran down her hand, already with the skinned knees, already with the fucking bike horns and her freckled nose, already with the trill of her southern Swedish Rs and her strange arrival through the hedge. You know, I say at last and get up to go to the bus, I just came here to visit my grandmother one last time, that's all, this was never supposed to happen, you're the one who came to me, and I can't help that it is what it is. That's your justification, she says, that it is what it is, is that really all you have to say, as if that explains anything and I say that yes, I don't have anything else to say except that there's nothing that can be done, that this is how it is and she and I, that I can call her Caroline, I can call her cousin, I can call her bunny, I can like her in this way but not in another, and by the way, I do know where the hollyhocks come from, they come from seeds, just seeds, why can't you just get that into your head.

The Swedish Series
from Readux Books

featuring stories by
three of Sweden's most exciting
contemporary authors

Malte Persson • *Fantasy*
Cilla Naumann • *The Lesson*
Amanda Svensson • *Where the*
Hollyhocks Come From

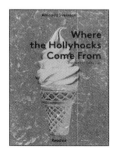

BOOKS & BEER

As the most literary brewery in America, we pride ourselves on our witty vernacular, whip-smart repartee, and widely-acclaimed library of published work. As a literal brewery, we also happen to make delicious beer. There's nothing quite as stimulating as a flavorful Brooklyn Brewery beer enjoyed with an excellent book.

Open up both for a wonderful pairing.

The Brooklyn Brewery 79 N 11th St, Brooklyn, NY 11249 • BrooklynBrewery.co
Facebook.com/TheBrooklynBrewery • @BrooklynBrewery • BrooklynBloggery.co

Literary Death Match

"...the most entertaining reading series ever."
— LA Times

Featuring:
4 brilliant authors
3 all-star judges
2 electric rounds
1 epic finale
(and a bunch of really attractive lit nerds)

Now in over 50 cities worldwide
and coming to a post code near you

@litdeathmatch #discoverLDM
www.LiteraryDeathMatch.com

Amanda Svensson

Amanda Svensson's debut novel, *Hey Dolly*, made her Sweden's most acclaimed author of 2008. Her second novel, *Welcome to This World*, was published in 2011 and shortlisted for the August Prize with the praise, "it's intense, it's innovative and it's utterly wonderful." Her latest novel, *All Those Things I Said to You Were True*, was published in March 2014 and completes her trilogy about three young women and their defiant attitude toward identity and the outside world. In addition to writing fiction, Svensson works as a cultural journalist. She was born in 1987 and lives in Malmö.